MRS LT

Weekly Reader Children's Book Club presents

A COLT NAMED *MISCHIEF*

by
Sandy Rabinowitz

Doubleday & Company, Inc.
Garden City, New York

LIBRARY OF CONGRESS CATALOGING IN PUBLICATION DATA
Rabinowitz, Sandy.
A Colt Named Mischief.
SUMMARY: Sara's father decrees
her mischievous young colt must go.
Two cattle thieves change his mind.
1. Horses—Legends and stories.
[1. Horses—Fiction] I. Title.
PZ10.3.R114Co [E]
Library of Congress Catalog Card Number 78-24779
ISBN: 0-385-14628-0 Trade
ISBN: 0-385-14629-9 Prebound
Copyright © 1979 by Sandy Rabinowitz
All rights reserved
Printed in the United States of America

To Mike, Abbie, Becca, David, and Mary

Mischief was a young colt who lived up to his name.
He was always causing trouble on the farm.

He liked to pluck chickens

and chase dogs.

He knocked over
buckets full of milk.

He bothered the pigs.

Sara loved Mischief. He was her colt.
She didn't mind if he shredded the laundry
or chewed on her hair.

But Sara's father did.

"Sara," he said, "can't you teach that colt some manners?"

"Oh, don't worry, Dad," said Sara. "Mischief is just curious about everything, and he chews because he's teething. When he gets older, he'll be a good farm horse."

"I hope you're right," said her hard-working father. "So far, he's been no help at all. He's just been a big bother."

"See what I mean! Tie Mischief up or I'll have to sell him."

Sara tied Mischief to a strong maple tree in the yard.
She felt sorry for him because he couldn't run free.

Mischief was bored. There was nothing to do, so he chewed and chewed on his rope until he had chewed right through it!

Soon he found something much better to chew on.
Sara caught him eating corn in the corncrib.
"Oh, no!" she cried. "You'd better get out of there
before Dad sees you."

But it was too late. "That's it!" yelled her father.
"I've had enough! I told you to keep that colt tied up.
Tomorrow he goes."

Sara pleaded, "Please let Mischief stay.
He won't get loose again."

But her father wouldn't listen.
Mischief had caused him too much trouble.
Sara's father locked him in the barn
for the night.

"Oh, Mischief," Sara sobbed as she fed him his supper,
"why couldn't you stay tied up? Now Dad's going to sell you.
I'll never see you again."

But Mischief didn't understand.
He just nibbled her sleeve as if nothing were wrong.

Mischief ate his hay slowly.
When he was finished,
he looked out the window.
The barnyard was quiet.

As he stood watching the dark road, he saw
a strange pick-up truck drive in through the gate.

Mischief was curious. He wanted to play
with the men who got out of the truck.
He didn't know they were cow thieves.

He pushed and nuzzled the bolt
on his door until it slid open.

He walked through the yard
to the strange truck.
He wondered which part
would be most fun to bite.

While the thieves were rounding up cows,
Mischief was chewing the truck's rubber tires.

When the thieves returned with two fat cows,
they noticed that one of their tires was flat.

Then, as one of the thieves looked for the spare tire,
Mischief made a rear-end attack!

The thief tried to escape, but Mischief was right behind him. "Help!" cried the man. "We can't get away! Quick! Get up on the truck."

Sara's father heard the shouting.
He ran out to see what was wrong.

When he saw what had happened, he laughed!
"Maybe Mischief's not a bad horse after all.
He's been a good watchdog tonight."

After the thieves were arrested and taken to jail,
Sara's father patted Mischief for the first time . . .

and Sara knew that Mischief could stay.